THE LIBRARY
OF LOST SOULS

Jenny Ringo and the House
of Fear: Book One

Chris Regan

www.jennyringo.com

THE FURTHER ADVENTURES OF JENNY RINGO...

Please visit **www.jennyringo.com** to find out more about the series.

If you would like to be kept up to date on future releases please sign up to the mailing list.

By signing up to the list you will be able to watch three free Jenny Ringo movies.

JENNY RINGO

THE LIBRARY OF
LOST SOULS

1: HALFWAY UP THE LIBRARY STAIRS

The student halfway up the library stairs was crying. I didn't want to see people crying in the library. The library was my sanctuary. It was my temple. It was my ... something else holy and important-sounding. I spent at least six hours in there every day. It was entirely unnecessary, I'm a terrible student and would mostly wander the shelves looking for something more interesting to read than whatever I was supposed to be reading. I'd chosen to study English Literature at Sussex Uni by mistake. The English Lit part was the mistake, I'd chosen Sussex Uni on purpose to move as far away from Stoke-on-Trent as possible and to make the city of Brighton my new adopted home. I hadn't really been all that bothered about what I studied so I'd gone for this combination Cultural/Media/

English Studies thing that would mean I would get to study/play video games and study/watch movies as well as learning about cultural hegemony and post-structuralism (I don't know what either of those things mean, they just come up in seminars a lot and the posh, *University Challenge* contestant students nod sagely whilst I pretend to be busy writing notes so no one will ask me a direct question).

Anyway, in the interview for the course, the fact that I only knew about video games and the street-dance movies of the early 2000s was beginning to count against me. Then the ancient professor bloke leading the interview asked me to compare a classic work of literature to a more modern one and I ran with the first two titles that popped into my head; Bram Stoker's *Dracula* and Helen Fielding's *Bridget Jones's Diary*. Because I'd seen the films. So, I ran with this and this professor bloke was getting all excited, to the point that he basically answered the question for me.

"Yes, I suppose they are both written in the epistolary style," he started.

I nodded, although at the time I had no idea what he meant and thought it was something to do with horse racing. I rambled a bit more, "Bridget, she's a bit like a Dracula, isn't she?"

There was nowhere to go with this. I'd dropped the

ball. Then he picked the ball up again and scored a hole-in-one (I am awesome at sports metaphors).

"Yes, if you were to turn it around and look at it from Mark Darcy or even Daniel Cleaver's point of view..."

He'd used the full character names. He was a true fan. I'd struck gothic/rom-com gold by mistake. He didn't want to be talking about cultural hegemony either! He wanted to compare Bridget Jones to a vampire and he went ahead and did that for a full half an hour. Then he shook my hand and said it had been the greatest of pleasures talking to me!

I passed the interview but I messed up my A-levels and didn't get the grades for the course where I could watch movies and play video games until someone asked me to compare two random titles at which point I would be hailed as the god of all media students and sent to be on *University Challenge*, at which point my claim to godhead would be questioned due to my poor performance and I would cry on national TV. Which would mean I would have to leave the country.

But when I was on the phone to the Admissions Department begging for a place, they mentioned that the old professor bloke had pretty much guaranteed me a place in his notes but that I should be studying straight English Literature.

So, there I was, at the university I wanted to study at in the city I wanted to live in but forced to spend endless hours in the library trying to catch up on all the literary classics and theory I was supposed to be an expert in.

Also, I didn't like socialising. I didn't like people really. The whole student partying thing wasn't for me.

That's a lie but you don't want to hear about all this. There was a student on the stairs crying.

I'm not good with criers. I never know what to say when someone starts dropping tears and snot in front of me. I think it's because I know that if I were crying in public, which would happen never, I would not want anyone to draw attention to my open display of emotional misery so I assume everyone else feels the same and would prefer me to leave them to it. I also wonder, sometimes, if it's just for attention and so I don't feel it's healthy for them for me to acknowledge the crying but better to just let them get over it and pull themselves together on their own. Really it's not either of those reasons, it's because I don't know what to do and I get all hot and shaky and I don't want to draw attention to that in case that prompts me to start crying and then I'd never be able to show my face again.

I worked in a chicken factory for a week the summer before I started uni. To clarify, they didn't make the chickens, they just sorted them. And killed them and stuff but I quit before they made me work in that bit. I quit because watching the endless parade of dead chickens pass over my head for seven hours a day five days a week brought on an epic existential crisis that threatened to swallow me whole if I didn't leave that place immediately.

That was my failed attempt at saving money for uni, which is one of the reasons I never went out. Not the main one but one of them.

In the chicken factory I used to work with a lady, we'll call her Joanne. Because that was her name. I don't think she's reading this. The existential crisis would certainly have eaten her soul by now.

One day I had a work-related question and decided to pose this question to my more experienced colleague, Joanne.

"Esteemed colleague, Joanne," I probably said, "Should one of these fine de-feathered, dead animals slip from my hands and land on the disease-smelling factory floor is it correct that I should pick said bird up and throw it back with the others? I was so instructed by our eminent foreman, Steve, and while I'm hesitant to question the will of Steve I am curious as to why such a practice is deemed acceptable?

Also, I've just noticed I dropped a chicken on the floor and it's been there for ages so..."

It was so loud in the factory it didn't really matter what I said as Joanne wouldn't have heard me anyway. However, when she turned to look at me, I noticed she was crying.

As if on cue we stopped for lunch and the machines were switched off so now Joanne's sobbing was quite clearly audible.

"Pardon, Gavin?" she asked between sobs, "I didn't catch that."

Gavin is my name, by the way, she didn't just randomly call me Gavin because she was so distraught she had forgotten who I was and just decided to call me Gavin because it was the first name that came into her head, or perhaps you were thinking it was the name of the lost love who had caused her distress in that moment, but it wasn't, it's my name, I had just forgotten to tell you that, or rather I hadn't forgotten I just couldn't find a neat way to slide it in there so I was going with ignoring it, until now.

I didn't ask Joanne what was wrong. I didn't even tell her my query wasn't all that important. I pretended we were all fine and I repeated my question and she had to tell me about floor-chicken procedures while crying her eyes out over whatever it was she was upset about (it was probably the fact that she'd taken a summer job in a chicken factory six years ago and had only just realised that this was her life forever now, which would make me cry too).

The moment had haunted me ever since and so when I saw the student halfway up the stairs to the third floor and I noted that she was crying I decided to contravene years of precedent and actually ask her whether I could help.

"Excuse me," I said, "Is there anything I can do to help?"

She sat in the middle of the step, her knees bunched up to her chin and supporting her hands, which she was using to entirely cover her face. This was rather an obvious sign that like me she did not want her tears exposed in public but, then why stop halfway up the stairs? It really was the most inconvenient place to sit, for everyone else at least.

"Are you all right?" I tried again.

She continued to sob.

I sat down next to her. The stairway was empty, by the way. It was 9pm on a Friday evening so not many of Sussex Uni's finest had the inclination to study but I didn't want to be out with the masses celebrating the end of another week of doing nothing so there I was, but you know that about me already (also that I lie about how much I really do want to spend time with people but you'll pick that up too eventually).

I decided on one final attempt at intervention before I left her to it.

I cleared my throat, mostly so she would have some idea of what was coming and could stop me if desired. I really hoped she would stop me but I was committed now.

"Halfway up the stairs is the stair where I sit," I sang, "There isn't any other stair quite - like - it."

She continued to cry but I felt if I stopped then it would have been super-awkward so I continued.

"It's not at the bottom. It's not at the top. So, this is the stair where I always stop."

The sound of footsteps on the stairs below me suddenly brought the situation crashing into focus. I was an insane person. I'm the one who normally assumes everyone wants to be left alone. Turns out I was right! Why on earth I had thought sitting next to a crying stranger and then singing would be perceived as anything other than supremely creepy I have no idea.

I stood and began to stride up the stairs two at a time to reach my destination as quickly as humanly possible.

I did, however, stop and turn to look at the sobbing student before I moved out of view and was mortified to see she had lifted her head from her hands and turned to look at me. However, my embarrassment was soon replaced with startled confusion when I saw that she didn't appear to have a face.

2: EYES WITHOUT A FACE (AND ALSO EYES)

I only saw the faceless student for a split-second so I put it down to a trick of the light. You can't cry so much it liquifies your entire face can you? That's just not a thing that happens. I resumed my usual Friday night library routine, which was the same as my usual anytme library routine, I just felt I should point out that it was Friday night again. Oh hang on, it's not an important plot point, don't mis-understand me, I'm not trying to draw attention to the fact that it was a Friday so you remember it for later, it's just a character beat, you know? I'm a guy who is more likely to be in a library on a Friday night rather than out partying or whatever, that's all. Sorry, I'm over-explaining, I do that a lot so will also try to stop apologising for it, which I also do a lot.

Here's how my library routine worked. I would head to the third floor, English Literature, because I was an English Literature student no matter how much I was in denial about it. I would then half-heartedly search for whatever books related to what I was supposed to be studying that semester. That week we were studying Godwin's The Adventures of Caleb Williams (I actually finished that one, pretty good book) and its roots in late 18th-century politics, but that meant going up to History on the next floor. The history students would stare at me like they knew I wasn't one of them (also I might see the stoner who lived in the same halls as me, the one with dreadlocks who wore the same Nirvana hoodie every day but seemed too posh to be into 90's grunge, his name was Daniel Middleton but I wasn't supposed to know that because we didn't actually know each other I'd just done some semi-casual stalking, and seeing him would be bad because I would probably say something embarrassing, like did he know the Nirvana bassist Krist Novoselic is a Trump supporter, and then have to spend the rest of the semester in my room afraid to come out in case I saw him again which would put an end to me tailing him to campus every day which some days was the only reason I was able to get out of bed in time for my first lectures so you see if I saw Daniel Middleton in the library it would pretty much mean the end of my entire academic career) so I parked that one for now. Then there was my Romantics class, we were reading William Blake that week so I was hoping I'd at least get to look at some pictures. And then there was my class on Post-War Absurdism, probably the one I needed the most help with. I couldn't find anything on the reading list for that one so I gave up and just started looking for the books with the weirdest titles instead, which is what I always ended up doing anyway.

Some ten minutes later I had a book about the Ten Saddest Clowns, another all about Cheese in 18th Century Literature, and perhaps most interesting, a copy of the Codex Seraphinus (which was my go-to weird book of choice to the point that I'd discreetly hidden it in the wrong section so no one else could take it out). I took said books to the most empty-looking table in the most deserted area of the library (not hard to find at 9.15pm on a Friday evening). Once seated I looked through the books in search of pictures and strange facts with which I could impress my friends but mostly pictures. I would do this for half an hour and then I'd get bored and explore the other floors (not History because Daniel Middleton) and do the same there. All told I could probably kill between two to four hours in the library on a night like that one if I was really trying.

So, there I was, reading about Alfonso Pasolucci, the saddest clown in the whole of 19th century Italy, when the worst thing that could possibly happen at that moment happened. Another student sat at the table (it's not Daniel Middleton so I guess it's the second-worst). This meant it was all over. I couldn't possibly enjoy the eclectic illustrations of the Codex Seraphinus with someone else in such close proximity. What if they spoke to me? I'd have to run away and then I'd have to exclude this whole floor of the library from my studies and as it's the English Lit floor and I'm an English Lit student that would make things a little difficult (actually it wouldn't have made any difference at all and may even have been a good thing but in the moment it felt like it would be a massive problem).

Once I had to use the computer room on campus and another student sat next to me and out of the corner of my eye I thought it was someone I knew so I said "Hello". To this day I'm not sure if we genuinely didn't know each other or whether she was just pretending but either way, she ignored me and when I pressed further, she said, "Sorry, I don't know you." She didn't even do the polite thing of pretending to know me enough to say "hello", which is what I would have done. I never used a computer on campus again after that.

Anyway, this student sat down opposite me but I'd only been there two minutes so I couldn't get up right away. I had to at least think of a mime I could do that made it look like I'd forgotten something so I could excuse myself without making it look like I was doing so because of the student sitting down opposite me. All the while I was thinking this I could feel him looking at me. I say 'him', I hadn't looked up at his face but the hands looked male, although that's probably unfair as he may not have identified as male but as I didn't ask him we'll go with the perhaps incorrect assumption I had at the time that this was a male student sitting in front of me. I could see his hands across the table and I could also see that he had no books in front of him. He wasn't making any effort to take any books or notes or even a laptop from his bag, his hands were just there on the table in front of him, and by extension in front of me. So, he'd sat down and wasn't doing anything other than possibly no probably definitely staring at me. I gave it another thirty seconds or so, actually it was exactly thirty seconds because I counted and it felt like an eternity. Then I looked up and there he was and my planned needing-a-wee mime went out the window.

He didn't have a face.

Imagine your face, okay? Then imagine you've taken an eraser and just rubbed out all the features, so the mouth, the eyes, the nose, any definition like cheekbones and wrinkles, all gone. The hair and ears are still there and the shape is there but the face bit, what we would think of when we say 'face', that's all gone. There's just this mass of flesh in the vague shape of a face. That's what he looked like.

What's going on? I imagine you're thinking that. You thought this would be a romance story about me pursuing Daniel Middleton, being ultimately rejected but then finding love in the most unlikely of places, like the faceless student sitting opposite me (if he had a face), he could have been the guy to whom I am Daniel Middleton and that was why he was being weird and I didn't get it because I was so obsessed with Daniel Middleton I didn't recognise my own stalkerish behaviour being reflected back at me, at least not until the end of the story where I'm about to kill myself (no wait that's too much) I'm about to move back to Stoke-on-Trent (which is the same, possibly worse) and then this guy finds me and I realise he loves me and maybe I could love him back and it all works out. It could have been that story if not for the fact that the student sitting opposite me being weird had no face.

Did you ever see the film *Stalker*? Andrei Tarkovsky made it in Russia in 1979. It's in the future except it doesn't look like the future, it looks like Russia in 1979, but it's set in the future and there are these three blokes, there's the Stalker, the Writer, and the Professor, and they go on this expedition to this place called THE ZONE, which looks like everywhere else but the characters talk about it like it's super dangerous. There's this scene when they first get to THE ZONE where the Stalker starts tying bits of white cloth to nuts and then chucking them into a field because that's the only way to make sure you're following the correct path in THE ZONE, except there's nothing to indicate what will happen if they stray from the path, you just have to take his word for it but really it's pretty obvious you're just watching three men throwing nuts in a field. I suspect this is where most people decide either to go along with the film and whatever other far-fetched scenarios Tarkovsky is going to suggest without actually showing (and there are many many more), or to switch it off and never find out what happens when the men encounter THE ROOM or THE MEAT GRINDER (the answer is not much but anyone who's made it to THE MEAT GRINDER scene knows that by then you've convinced yourself Stalker is the greatest film ever made because it has to be because if it's not you just spent three hours watching men throwing nuts in a field).

This is the throwing nuts in a field moment. I know it's happening early but here it is. You could put this book down (or switch off your device or whatever) and never find out where the faceless students come from and that's okay because you don't really care, you thought this was a slightly disturbing romance novel about inappropriate stalking (which, incidentally, doesn't happen at all in the film *Stalker*), so you'd be forgiven for giving up at the point that the people with no faces turn up. However, those of you who go along with it are in for a very strange adventure, I can promise you that.

I'll wait while you decide.

I should've gone with the moment in *Solaris* where there's a shot of a guy sitting in silence in a car that goes on for like twenty-minutes because that's a real test of your faith in Tarkovsky but it's too late now.

Done?

Okay, those of you who are still here, let's continue.

I made a kind of 'yelping' noise and recoiled in horror which resulted in me pushing my chair back until it fell over and I toppled off onto the floor. The faceless man stood up and stepped towards me. I was not going to wait around to see what he would do so I untangled my legs from the chair and crawled away. As soon as I was able, I stood up and ran.

I ran right into another faceless student, colliding hard enough to send me to the floor again. The student tried to help me up and not thinking I took their hand but once they'd pulled me up, they wouldn't let go. They were pulling me towards them and I could see the other student from the table coming up behind me.

This was all happening very, very quickly and I

17

was kind of acting on impulse. I wasn't scared at this point. It's like when you cross the road whilst listening to true crime podcasts and it's a really interesting bit where they're reading the autopsy report or whatever so you're concentrating on that and don't notice you're about to step out in front of an oncoming vehicle until the last second at which point you manage to stop just in time but then afterwards you realise you were nearly hit by a car and should probably pay more attention when crossing roads, although if you haven't learnt that by the time you're a grown-up there's not much hope for you. The scary part is the thought of how close you came to death, not the car nearly hitting you because in the moment you were acting on pure adrenaline. That's like what this was. My body knew I was in danger and was doing the running and stuff, which was handy because I was mostly still trying to work out what had happened to their faces.

I managed to wriggle free and headed for the sanctuary of the shelves, which was in hindsight a huge mistake because if a student had been coming in the opposite direction, I wouldn't have room to get past and would potentially be blocked in. Which is exactly what happened.

So now there's this faceless student in front of me, arms outstretched as if she's trying to grab me (I'm saying this one was definitely a she but happy to be corrected if you were in fact the student in question). I turned around and there's the student who grabbed me and the one who sat at the table. Three of them.

I considered my options and decided if I was going to escape it would be via the path of least resistance i.e. the single student in front of me. I rushed her hoping to tackle her to the floor but we just kind of bumped into each other then lost our balance and both fell over.

"Pin her down!" said a voice from above.

I looked up and that's when I saw Jenny Ringo for the first time.

3: HERE'S WHAT COULD BE HAPPENING

I really hate it in books when there's too much describing things. I feel like I should just be able to say "20s, goth/emo, tattoos" and you should get it and move on but then I also feel like this is the title character I'm describing so technically I owe you more of a description than that, but descriptions of characters in books always make me feel a bit nauseous. She had a perfect oval face with alluring almond-shaped eyes and a sharp but graceful nose. That's not at all what she looked like, I'm just giving you an example of the stuff that makes me feel nauseous. It's never genuine; it's never, "she had one of those weird-looking faces that makes you think they're always giving you a funny look when really it's just their face," it's always like the author chose a rounded geometric shape and added some stuff, like they're literally doing a Mr. Potato Head and describing the process. Unless they're a bad character, then it will all be about how there's darkness behind their eyes or how their fondness for chocolate has led to excess weight in unsightly places, which really is all of us but in books it's always the characters we're not supposed to like. And don't say it's not all books, I'm sure it's not, but I've read loads, I've read *The Adventures of Caleb Williams* and the *Ten Saddest Clowns* so I know all about books and stuff.

Let's go with her clothes, I suppose I can give you that. She was wearing these heavy, black boots, like work boots, for people who do work with machinery and walking across nails and stuff I guess, and she had these stripy tights, thick black and red stripes like she was a Dark World Dr. Seuss character. She had this black dress that was frayed at the hem, not on purpose but like she'd literally been wearing the same dress every day for a year. She had maybe four or five pendants of varying lengths around her neck, each with some kind of pop-occult symbol like a pentagram, probably an ankh and a few others I didn't recognise. Her hair was long, black and streaked with purple. There were tattoos all over her arms but not like a sleeve, these were individual small images and symbols that I would later learn were intended to be more practical than decorative (ooh, slipped in a future plot point too, killing this writing thing! Note to me – Remember to refer to this later on otherwise it will seem pretty stupid on multiple reads. Note to the person re-reading the whole series for the eighth time – you know whether I remembered to refer to this again or not, how did I do?)

It should go without saying (but I'm saying it anyway for the sake of clarity) that all of the above details were picked up after the fact. The other thing I hate about descriptions in books is where there's a really long description of something or somebody in an intense moment and you think, "Oh sure, you just stopped to take all of that in, right?" One of my overall life anxieties (filed under, "Things that will probably never happen but I will worry about happening anyway") is that I'll be witness to some kind of crime and then Angela Lansbury or Quincy or Dr. Dick Van Dyke or whoever will ask me what happened and I won't remember because who remembers details like that? You know, when the witnesses on TV are all like, "He was 5'11" with reddish-brown hair and maybe weighed 110 pounds" – how the fuck can you tell someone's weight and height from looking at them? I mean, maybe that is possible for some people but not for me. How do you even practice that? It's not like you're at a party and you say, "Hey, I'm going to guess your weight!" because whether you get it right or wrong it's probably going to get you thrown out (inappropriate party etiquette is another anxiety I have despite not really going to enough parties for it to be a legitimate concern). The point is my memory is pretty bad, even if I did take a moment to properly absorb this person's (who we all know is Jenny so I'm just going to call her Jenny even though in the story she hasn't introduced herself yet but you can catch up) appearance and attire I probably wouldn't have remembered it later so let's just accept the above description is from observations compiled over a some time, not just in the moment. I mean she pretty much wore the same outfit every day, except maybe changing the colour of the tights or wearing a slightly different frayed black dress so just put that picture of Jenny in your head and keep it there.

At that moment I couldn't take that in because a student with no face was trying to get me, although maybe I had been staring at her for longer than I thought because then she shouted, "Do it!"

I was on my knees, the student on the floor was reaching for the shelves to try to pull herself up. Behind me, the two other faceless students were ambling (having no face seemed to slow them down) ever nearer. I understood Jenny's instruction but it was taking longer than usual for the thought to bloom into action.

Then, a moment of clarity.

"Is this one of those immersive theatre things?"

I mean it seemed like the kind of thing that might happen. I should explain.

23

So back in the day, there was LARPing (I'll wait while you Google it) where people would pretend they were playing D&D but in real life, which I could never figure out because D&D was all based on dice rolls so when you're dressed up as a knight and you run into a bloke dressed up as a goblin do you both take out the dice and roll to see who wins? Or do you hit each other with plastic swords until one of you gives up? You probably already know more about this than I do from Googling it, everything I know is from that Tom Hanks film where he loves LARPing so much he goes crazy and thinks there are real monsters (it's a real film, Google it). So, you have that, and then you also have the Theatre of Cruelty, popularised by Antonin Artaud who said things like, "All writing is garbage. People who come out of nowhere and try to put into words any part of what goes on in their minds are pigs." Which is irrelevant, I just like the quote. He also said, "We are not free. And the sky can still fall on our heads. And the theatre has been created to teach us that first of all." So, he's saying life is pretty fucked-up and we can prove it to people by fucking with them in theatre, which Artaud did by making people sit on the floor, removing any notion of personal space and using lighting and sound to basically irritate as much as possible. You mash Theatre of Cruelty with LARPing and you get immersive theatre – actors fucking with their audience and invading personal space on the understanding that they have somehow consented to this torture because they are also playing a part, except they aren't really because they don't know what's going on and there are no dice. It's interactive storytelling for people who don't play videogames. That's what I thought was happening in the library.

"I've got a great idea," says Julian at the end of a Drama seminar on Artaud and the Theatre of Cruelty, "Why don't we put on an impromptu immersive theatre piece in the library?"

"That's a great idea!" says Bunny enthusiastically (her real name isn't Bunny but there's a story there, just don't get her started because the rest of us have heard it a million times), "We could pretend to have no faces and go after people who come in. It will be a comment on the loss of individuality due to the oversubscription to mass-marketed undergraduate study."

"We could film it and submit it as our final exam piece!" says Baxter, who applied to do film studies but so impressed the interview panel with his comparison between Benjamin Johnson and *Bob the Builder* that he ended up taking Drama by mistake.

"And we can also really fuck with people!" says no one although they're all thinking it.

So it was with some measure of relief that I clambered on top of the faceless student and attempted to pin her to the ground (which I'm not really strong enough to do) and I disregarded her attempts to claw out my eyeballs as the controlled movements of a perhaps slightly over-enthusiastic actor.

"I'm afraid it's not immersive theatre," said Jenny, "They just really want your face."

As a direct response to this new information I fully committed to pinning the student to the floor as I now feared if I loosened my grip on her wrists, she would in fact claw my eyes out.

Jenny dropped down from the shelves and straddled the prone student, her thighs clamping the faceless head in place. With some of the pressure off keeping that student from escaping, I looked over my shoulder at the two approaching from behind. Luckily in their eagerness to get at me they seemed to have become tangled up in each other's arms and were rocking back and forth in this weird, faceless dance that made the whole situation seem even more like a performance art piece. The commotion was attracting attention though and I could hear the footsteps of more presumably faceless students shuffling towards our row.

Jenny had this bag over her shoulder, big and made with this tattered, fluffy black material that didn't seem at all practical suggesting she'd probably made it herself. There were badges all over the bag for various bands I'd never heard of at the time and writing this now I wish I'd never heard of still. She fumbled around and took out a thick, black permanent marker pen.

Taking the cap in her mouth Jenny proceeded to draw on the prone faceless student's face, more specifically she drew a smiley face in the space where the student's face should have been. The pen made this awful squeak as it slid along the unusually smooth flesh, but it was over in a second and now the formerly faceless student had a face again, albeit a supremely goofy face, like a child had drawn it but that's not a reflection on Jenny's art skills, as you can imagine she was in a bit of a rush.

"Okay," she announced as she stood up slowly, "Let her go!"

I was barely holding her anyway although the violent reaction from the faceless student as I moved away suggested perhaps I'd had a greater hold than I thought. She sat up clumsily, reaching for me as she had done before. I'd naively thought that the drawing of the face had been some sort of temporary cure for the unusual ailment but apparently it wasn't that simple.

"Cover your face!" shouted Jenny as she manoeuvred away from the scrabbling student and out from the shelves.

I covered my face with my hands, peeking only to see where I was going as I sidestepped away from my attacker. The student was on her feet already and indeed covering my face had seemed to slow her down. Then I understood the intended effect of drawing the crude face on her faceless head. The two students behind her having untangled themselves from each were now on the move again, but they were no longer coming for me, they were going for the student with the marker-pen face.

I watched as the two students clawed their prey to the ground grabbing at her temporary smile until I felt someone nudge me with an elbow. It was Jenny and she motioned to follow. Briefly noticing that the 3rd floor of the library was now full of faceless students I decided following the one person who a) still had a face and b) seemed to know what she was doing about all this was probably my best option for survival.

Looking back, I wonder if all this could have been avoided had I simply taken my chances and run from the library at that moment. What is that version of me doing now all these years later? I imagine my brush with death would have given me a renewed sense of purpose and the knowledge I was perhaps living on borrowed time would lead me to take risks and challenge myself in a way pre-faceless-library-massacre me would never have dreamed of. Perhaps I would have crossed paths with Daniel Middleton on the way back to my room and I would have seized the moment and asked if he wanted to go for a drink. And now we're living together and he's a lawyer and I'm a video games journalist and we have this super-expensive apartment in London but at the weekend we retreat to our Brighton flat overlooking the sea. We have our ups and downs like all couples but for the most part, we're really very happy. When people ask how we met Dan tells this hilarious version of the story where I ran out of the library like a crazy person and practically leapt into his arms, which he thought was weird at first but he could see something was troubling me so he agreed to go for a drink with me and by our third round we fell in love. It's a great story until someone asks, "What was it that was troubling you?" and I have to lie about some assignment I was worried about and hope they don't ask for details because I can't remember what I said the last time someone pressed me for more information and I don't want Dan to catch me lying. Once, over an anniversary dinner, we had a huge fight about my reluctance to talk about what happened that night so he decided never to bring it up again, but the fact that he doesn't know the whole truth keeps me awake some nights. Occasionally I wonder what became of the goth with the stripy tights who saved my life that night. What would have happened if I hadn't fled the library at all?

Well, I didn't flee the library so let's go back and find out.

4: CLEVER PUN ABOUT OVERDUE BOOKS AND MISSING FACES TO GO HERE

I followed Jenny to a table in the study area where she had scattered what looked like twenty-odd old looking books. Most of them were open and many of the yellowed pages were populated with intriguing diagrams and pictures. It looked like she'd found the one section of the library that had been used as part of a Harry Potter film set. They looked like movie-prop books, like they couldn't have actual writing on the pages beyond those that were open and in view, but they did, I checked. I also had a quick look to see if any of them had that Goya painting of Satan devouring his son as movies will always use that to denote creepy books but no, not a Satan in sight. The images that were there were unfamiliar and also more scientific than Satanic. It's like when I decided to be a Wiccan but then I Googled it and found out it's all a bit boring and you don't even get to sacrifice anything. I suppose I should have looked into Satanism instead where you do get to sacrifice things (or used to be able to, modern Satanists seem a bit boring so they probably don't do that anymore) but then I didn't really want to actually sacrifice things I just liked the idea of being part of a religion that did, but then really the idea of being part of any religion didn't sit well with me so I decided to abandon the whole venture. The books seemed more like instruction manuals anyway, just very old instruction manuals and instructing what I couldn't say. Mostly I was annoyed that this stranger had been hoarding all the interesting books in the library because this was exactly the kind of literature I would definitely have used to pretend I was doing actual work.

There was other stuff on the table too, some flowers and plants and a few things in jars. There were candles, currently unlit as I suspect lighting candles in the library isn't allowed but then I've never seen that actually stated anywhere. There was a weird curvy knife on the table that was borderline Halloween prop but equally looked sharp enough to be of questionable legality. And there was this one larger, oldest looking book that Jenny seemed to be most interested in. She was flicking through the pages and then consulting her handwritten notes on an A4 refill pad amongst the clutter.

Again, this would have been a perfect opportunity to leave. However, looking around I saw more face-less students wandering aimlessly and the thought crossed my mind that perhaps I should obtain a bit more information on the circumstances. Was my face really in danger? Are their faces gone forever or just temporarily removed? Have they always been like this and if so, how do they get by every day? Has this always been a thing and I've just never heard of it (like that time someone explained Daylight Saving Time to me and I realised that my generally poor time-keeping had meant that for my first 18 years on this planet I'd just ignored it and some-how got by despite being an hour out of sync with most people for half the year)? Is this, in fact, some kind of support group meeting for people without faces and actually Jenny was a right-wing anti-face-less protestor and I was being inducted into a hate group? All these questions raced through my mind but I decided to start with the obvious one.

"What happened to them?"

Jenny looked up from her notes and seemed to think for a moment before she answered, "Mostly it was an accident."

I'll let Jenny tell this next part because I wasn't there and if I told it I'd have to add more detail and then you'd think, "Wait, there's no way all this detail would be in the story she told you," and you'd be correct, well done you, but that's how fiction works isn't it? Suspension of disbelief and all that. Except I don't want to argue anymore so here's Jenny telling it in probably more detail than she told me at the time because at the time we were being surrounded by faceless students who wanted to eat us.

How do we do this?

Dear reader, please note that the role of the narrator will now be performed by Jennifer Ringo.

Thanks. What is it you want me to do?

Tell them the story. About how the library thing started.

I thought this was your thing?

It is. I'll write down what you tell me and then this part can be in your words so it's accurate.

I don't really give a fuck if it's accurate or not. It's your memoir.

It's not a memoir it's ... I don't know what it is. It's like Sherlock Holmes, yeah? You're Holmes, I'm Watson, you go on adventures, I chronicle them. It's a chronicle. I'm a chronicler.

At no point did Watson say, "I wasn't there for this bit. Holmes, you have a go at the chronicling."

He might have done. I never read any.

Fair point, me neither. Okay. Which part?

The library. How it all started.

It started with that prick librarian who wouldn't give me a job!

Yes, that part. From the top.

I wasn't a student there. Have you explained that?

No, that's what I need you to do.

So, you want me to fill in the context as well? You basically want my fucking life story?

Fine, I'll start us off. You weren't a student. You came to the library that day looking for a job. You had an interview with the head librarian.

Keep going! You're doing great.

The interview didn't go well. The librarian gave you some helpful feedback.

He said I needed to do some growing up if I expected any-

one to give me a real grown-up job.
Really? That's what he said?

He said it in a more mansplainey way because he was a prick but basically, yeah.

And then he gave you a look. I remember you seemed to think that was important.

Yeah, he gave me this look like I was less than nothing. Like he was annoyed he'd wasted his time on me and that now he was done with me I wasn't even there as far as he was concerned.

And your reaction was?

You know this part.

I know but it was better the way you told it.

I just thought it would be interesting to see him try to give me that look if he didn't have a face.

And you basically took out the whole library by mistake!

You ruined the ending! But yeah, that's what happened. It was because of—

Whoa, hold on! Don't spoil the actual ending.

You just spoiled my fucking ending!

Yeah, but that's like a background story, it's not the main thing. All we need to know right now is that you cast a spell from your new book –

--That's all I was going to say! It was from my new book. Why haven't you mentioned the book?

I have mentioned it, I just didn't go into detail. Can you explain where the book came from?

This part I definitely told you.

I know but seeing as you're here let's have it in your own words, rather than me retelling the story you told me at a time of crisis.

I found this book in a second-hand bookshop. Probably the last second-hand bookshop in the country. It was one of those posh places where the guy looked at me over his glasses like he knew I couldn't afford anything, which was true.

So more like an antiquarian bookshop.

Am I not telling this to your satisfaction?

You're doing fine, I just think you should provide more detail because when you say "second-hand bookshop" dear reader is probably imagining the back room of a charity shop with a hundred copies of the same Danielle Steel book and nothing else.

Who's Danielle Steel?

I don't know. Maybe she's really good. There's always loads of her books in charity shops, that's all. Pick another example if you prefer. I just think you need to differentiate between that and the typical antiquarian bookshop which generally sells rare antique books like the ones that might be sought after by Johnny Depp in that film where Skeletor hires him to find the rarest book.

There is so much to unpack there.

It was an antiquarian bookshop. Please, continue.

So yeah, the guy is looking at me like he's about to kick me out and I'm not going to outright ask him for books on occult shit because that would be all the excuse he needed so I browse for a bit and he coughs a bit and then I think he's going to say something but I've found this one really old book. It was hidden behind some other books, that's where you have to look for the good shit. I pulled this book off the shelf and he suddenly looks all shocked like he thought he'd burned that book. In fact, he looked at me like he'd burned it, put it through a shredder, pissed on it and bathed it in acid and still there it was. If it was a film there would be like a montage of all this.

Depends who made the film. If it was like Godard or someone there would be a whole separate scene except he'd be dressed the same as in the previous scene so we wouldn't even realise it was a flashback until we watched a YouTuber explain it in a twenty-minute pseudo-academic explainer video afterwards. Or, if this was a big budget studio film the bookshop owner would simply point at the book and say, "That book! I thought I'd buried it!"

Let's just say he was surprised to see it and when I showed the vaguest of interests, he practically gave it away until he realised I'm an idiot and was going to pay him for it anyway so he gave it to me for a fiver.

And now you have the book.

Yes, and it's like the weirdest fucking book of spells. Not even conventionally weird, you know, when I say "weirdest fucking book of spells" I expect you think of unrecognisable writing and images of strange celestial beings with tentacles sketched in blood but it wasn't like that. It just felt weird. The first time I looked at it I thought the pages were blank and I thought I'd been ripped off. I didn't have chance to have a proper look though because I was late for my interview.

Which is why the librarian turned you down.

No, that's because he was a smug-faced prick. I decided I would see how he would find being a smug-faced prick with no face at all. So, I opened the book—

Okay, let's stop there. If you explain too much about the book, they'll figure out the ending. Also, it kind of makes it seem like you figured out what was going on when it was actually my genius idea that fixed everything.

That's not exactly true.

When we get to that part you can correct me but we have a lot of ground to cover before then.

So, you're done with me for now?

Yes, you run along and get on with whatever it was you were doing.

Are you sure you don't need more context? I've just turned up to your library casting spells and stuff. Do you want to know a bit about my background? How I learnt magic? My years at wizard school?

You didn't go to wizard school. Did you?

No, I don't think there is one. But maybe I did. These things and more you could learn if you did a deep dive into my history with magic.

You didn't want to do a deep dive! You didn't even want to tell me about the librarian.

Yeah, I changed my mind.

I'm sort of telling this from my point of view at the time, you know? So, there I am being a student, albeit a shitty one, and then you turn up with the faceless students and we're just in it. It's happening.

Okay. You seem to know how you want to tell this story.

I still want your input! We can go into more of your backstory later if you like.

No, I wouldn't want to spoil anything. You carry on.

She's pissed off with me now. Anyway, we'll go there in the end.

So, Jenny was there for an interview, the librarian was a bit rude, she decided to cast a spell from her new spell book that would take off the librarian's face because that's totally a normal reaction and a thing people do. Ah, actually there is one more thing I need Jenny to explain. Jen!

What? Oh, you want my backstory now? I suppose I first became interested in magic as a child watching this TV show called Breaking the Magician's Code where they explain how all the tricks work and I was heartbroken be-

cause I'd always thought maic was real. I decided from that moment on—

No, it's not that. I just need you to explain that you're shit at magic.

What the fuck?

It's important.

And not true.

I'm not judging.

This sounds very judgey.

Right, let me explain. You cast a spell to remove the librarian's face. Now, out of context, that sounds quite harsh.

I already explained, he was a prick!

I know, but still. Taking someone's face, that's some messed-up *Hellraiser* gubbins right there.

Gubbins?

You have to explain that you didn't know how the spell would work. You weren't thinking, "This will tear the flesh from the face in the bloodiest way possible," anymore than you were thinking, "This will leave him with a smooth fleshy pulp instead of a face." You didn't know. And it didn't matter that you didn't know because you are shit at magic.

Were. I were shit at magic. I mean I was shit at magic. I'm not anymore.

That's spoiler territory again! We'll get to all that. It's just that at this particular moment I think it's important to mention that when you opened the book and cast the spell you had no concerns about scarring the librarian for life because you didn't think it would work. Because nothing had ever worked.

Do you really need me to say it?

I think if the reader is going to have any sympathy for you going forward then yes, you need to say it.

Fine. I was shit at magic. I didn't think it would actually work. Nothing had ever worked until that day in the library with that book. Is that all?

Yes. Yes, that's rather good actually. Sort of hints at backstory without really giving too much away. Maybe you should be chronicling your own chronicles.

Fuck that, I can't be arsed. As you were.

Right, good, I'm glad we established that. So, thinking the spell wouldn't work Jenny whispered the words from her new spellbook into her hands and blew the magic out in the direction of the librarian's office. Thereafter she realised that everyone who had been in the library at that time was now missing a face and feeling a little guilty, mostly quite proud of herself, but guilty enough to want to put it right she came up to the third floor of the library in search of books that could help reverse the spell and that's where she met me.

"It's one of those LARPing things, isn't it? Where everyone runs around with plastic swords throwing flour?" I asked as Jenny finished telling me a much more succinct version of what she'd done to the library.

I looked around as if expecting to be hit by a bag of flour. I was in denial and was back on the LARPing/immersive theatre theory, like that Tom Hanks movie again but real and not just in my head, because it was the only thing that really made any sense. What I saw behind me was stranger than that movie existing and indeed stranger than anything that had happened so far that evening.

5: LITTLE LIBRARY OF HORRORS

S o, I used a bit of creative licence at the end of the last chapter, I didn't turn away from the table as a consequence of my LARPing theory it's just that the paragraph flowed better if I suggested I had. In reality, several things prompted me to turn around and I'm not entirely sure which one I noticed first. It could have been the horrified expression on Jenny's face (well not exactly horrified, it wasn't "teen in a slasher film having just seen the killer standing behind you with a machete" kind of horror, it was more, "oh, I was going to explain that this situation is actually a million times worse than you first thought but it looks like you're about to find that out for yourself" kind of horror). It could have been the sound of ceiling tiles being popped out of place and hitting the floor behind me, although I've never heard that happen before so I wouldn't have guessed that's what the sound was. It could have been the silhouette of something long and tentacle-ey snaking its way across the table in front of me (meaning the silhouette was on the table so the actual thing itself was behind me, in case I explained that badly. This part is really messed-up so it's important that you understand exactly what is happening.)

I turned around and was surprised and a little relieved to see the face of a student right next to mine. It looked like Dave Barr from Introduction to Cultural Studies. I didn't really know him very well, he wasn't a "friend" and I'm not sure he'd remember my name, but he'd made an impression because in that first seminar where everyone introduces themselves he let slip that he had been on the Olympic Fencing team for England, which was a bit of a dick move. Sure, very impressive and stuff and I guess it made him maybe 25% more attractive (I don't know, fencing is a bit of a twat's sport so I'll probably revise that figure later) but the point is the rest of us were saying things like, "My name is Gavin and my favourite cheese is Camembert" but you neglect to do a proper French pronunciation on Camembert so the rich kids laugh at you and while that's happening Dave Barr says, "I was on the Olympic Fencing Team. What do you think of that, cheese boy?" He didn't call me cheese boy, but he may as well have. The Camembert thing was supposed to be a joke, like "I don't know what to say, let's talk about cheese," but fuck Dave Barr for making me look like a dickhead.

Anyway, now his face is stuck to the end of a plant so things didn't work out so well for old Dave Barr. He won't be doing much Olympic-level fencing without arms or legs or a body. So yeah, that's what had happened, he was part tree now. The tree he was connected to was coming down from the ceiling, multiple branches poking through the ceiling tiles all across the third floor except they weren't like normal, static, non-moving tree branches (I know static and non-moving are the same thing but I'm going for emphasis) they were writhing and undulating and creeping like, well, like the tentacles of some giant octopus or something. At the end of each branch-tentacle was a different face. There was Emily Claflin who lived in the same halls as me. There was Rob DeMatteis who I spent my first night on campus with when we both couldn't get into the Fresher's Party and I suggested we get drunk to calm my crippling social anxiety so we did and we ended up sitting on his bed making out until the early hours of the morning but then he stopped speaking to me because reasons. Anyway, I won't introduce you to all of the faces because who cares but there were faces attached to this giant plant and they were faces of actual students at the university.

"Watch out!" shouted Jenny after the split-second it had taken me to think all of the above had zipped by.

I looked back to see Dave Barr open his mouth and try to bite me. He would've managed it if I hadn't been able to step back just in time. The other faces on stalks were coming after me too and they looked like they meant it.

What I hadn't noticed while all this was going on is that one of the tentacle branches had coiled itself around my ankle. I know you would think one would notice something like that, if only because of the physical pressure of something wrapping itself around a part of your body, but it happened very quickly and before I could really acknowledge that it had happened and then really interrogated myself on why I hadn't noticed it happening I was being held upside down and lifted up off the ground. By the giant plant thing coming from the ceiling with angry student faces attached to its tentacle-branches. The faceless students were still there, by the way. I know it feels like this has been going on for months because of my meandering narrative style but this really all happened over a matter of seconds.

"Should I cover my face?" I asked, it seeming like a logical question at the time.

"No," replied Jenny, "This one just wants to eat you."

Words you do not want to hear when suspended from the ceiling by your ankle, which is caught in the tentacle-branch of a giant plant that apparently lives in the ceiling of the third floor of the library. In case you were wondering, as I'm sure you must be, the face on the end of the branch that had my ankle belonged to Issy Floyd, head of the Creative Writing Society which I had joined knowing full well I would never attend a single meeting due to a crippling fear of sharing my writing in public even though, as you can tell, I am clearly the greatest author who ever lived. That's sarcasm. If I really were the greatest author who ever lived I would be able to put that across without having to explain it but I can't and that's why I won't be attending any Creative Writing Society meetings, but now I definitely won't be because Issy Floyd tried to bite off my kneecap and I'm not sure you can have a normal conversation with someone after something like that.

Despite the imminent death by chomping-face-on-a-tree, I'm ashamed to say I was more worried when I noticed Jenny rifling through the contents of my bag. I don't know what I was afraid she would find in there. My notepad that was mostly doodles of teddy bears wearing 3-piece suits? My Dib-Dabs (when I was I child I loved Dib-Dabs but was only allowed them on special occasions, like when my dad happened to have been in a shop that sold them, which was rare because not many shops sold them because they weren't very popular. I mean, they're essentially a bag of sugar with a stick of sugar to eat the sugar with, however, the rarity of the Dib-Dab meant that being of an age to buy Dib-Dabs freely I would do so with abandon, assuming I could find a source, and having found such a source at a newsagent on my way to the bus stop I would now take a Dib-Dab into the library as my secret library snack)? The pack of flavoured condoms I'd bought from a machine in a pub toilet on a dare when I was 15 that I now carried around "just in case" despite not really being confident they were still usable, but then I was also fairly confident I wouldn't need emergency condoms so carrying them around all the time was part of an unspoken agreement with my psyche, the agreement being we just wouldn't think about it too much? My copy of Retro Gamer Magazine issue 83, a magazine about defunct video game systems that I would buy copies of on eBay and read as if studying an ancient civilization (issue 83 included a feature on the history of Donkey Kong Country and an article on the making of classic dinosaur beat-em-up Primal Rage in case you were wondering)? My copy of Naked Lunch, the book I'd been carrying around since the sixth form because I thought reading it made me look cool and interesting but actually I'd never made it past the first 5 pages and didn't really want anyone to see it in case they asked me questions? There were many, many more things I would have been embarrassed for Jenny to find but I didn't have time to think of them all so I decided to ask the question –

"What are you looking for?"

Having emptied the contents of the bag out onto the floor Jenny picked up a spray-on deodorant and brandished it above her head like it was the holy grail.

"Boy stuff," she said.

Then she climbed up onto the table and sprayed a decent amount of Lynx Africa into Issy Floyd's eyes. Issy screeched in agony, which was a bit extra really. I'm sure having deodorant sprayed into your eyes isn't pleasant but the way she was screaming was like Jenny had plucked out her eyeball, run it across a cheese grater while it was still attached, doused it in vinegar and then re-inserted it into the socket. She hadn't done that, she just sprayed her with deodorant but the screeching went on forever and it seemed to be affecting the other faces too. I suppose that made sense, they were all connected, I just hadn't really processed that fact at the time and the sound of a dozen heads attached to a giant plant all screeching at once was rather alarming. It seemed to be doing the trick though as I felt the vine around my ankle loosen and shortly afterwards fell, landing on my head.

Jenny pulled me to my feet and we started to run.

I did look back for a second, wondering whether to go back for the Dib-Dab, but I could see the faces had recovered and were looking even more angry and bitey than before so I made the heartbreaking decision to let it go. Jenny was not so happy to relinquish her beloved leather-bound book, which she abandoned me to go back for once we were a safe distance from the plant. I watched as she danced between the lunging faces on vines and ceiling tiles above were punched out by more of them and all the while the faceless students lumbered across the third floor towards us, oblivious to the carnivorous plant above them. Seeing the faceless students and the plant made of faces at the same time provoked a question, which Jenny answered on her safe return.

"It's a faceplant. I was hoping I could grow their faces back. It didn't quite work."

6: WORMFOOD

More faces seemed to be descending from the ceiling by the second, suggesting the growing of faces was working just fine, it was their attitude that needed fixing. They certainly had little interest in donating their faces to the advancing horde of faceless students. More distressing was the fact that the nearest exit was now beyond a thick curtain of angry face-vines and faceless zombies. We were trapped.

Jenny spotted the rare book section at the end of the library. It didn't have anything all that rare on the shelves really, just older books in a small area enclosed within glass partitions with its own door. The door was supposed to be locked and students weren't supposed to take the books out but I think the librarians were bored of being asked for the key all the time by curious students like me looking for the strangest books in the library so had decided to leave it unlocked so everyone could see that the books it housed were boring and not worth anything on eBay. It didn't look like the best hiding place, being see-through and all that, but Jenny was already on her way and we didn't appear to have many more options available to us.

Jenny shut the door behind me as I followed her in and a face slammed up against the glass. As it tried unsuccessfully to eat its way through I realised that had I been a second slower it would have been munching the back of my head but I decided it would be best not to dwell on such thoughts and put it to one side to traumatise me later. Jenny laid her book on the table in the room and started to flick through the pages, frantic. I pushed one of the other tables up against the door, which seemed to be enough to prevent the plant from pushing the door open.

"Okay, let's think about this," she said like it was a brainstorming session in a GCSE Business Studies task, "What kills plants?"

"Bugs?" I replied immediately because I secretly quite enjoyed brainstorming sessions. I'd always been quite good at saying the first words that came into my head without thinking them through.

"Good! Now, what type of bug will we find in a library?"

"I don't know ... a bookworm?"

See, I told you. Jenny thought I was serious and started flicking through the pages of her book again. I decided I had to put a stop to this, the face-plant would break through the glass soon, we needed a real plan, we couldn't waste time researching my bullshit ideas.

"Wait, I wasn't being serious."

"No, I think you're onto something."

I opened my mouth to protest once more but Jenny had opened the book to a particular page and turned it to show me. There, among Hammer horror-looking symbols and words written in a language I didn't recognise, there was a woodcut image of a prehistoric worm creature emerging from the pages of a book (a picture of a book inside a book, which was pretty meta for what appeared to be a medieval spellbook). It looked like a tapeworm but ... actually, I've never seen a real tapeworm. It looked like what I imagine tapeworms look like in my worst nightmares although there's no point me describing what the picture looked like because I'm going to have to describe the real thing soon enough. The point is, it didn't look very friendly and I wasn't entirely sure how helpful it would be to our cause but Jenny didn't seem concerned.

"Bookworms aren't an actual thing, are they?" I tried one last time.

It was a little late for this type of question because although the glass door didn't shatter, as predicted, it was instead being ripped off its hinges by one of the tentacle-like vines.

"Let's find out!" said Jenny and then she cupped her hands in front of her mouth, whispered something indecipherable into her palms then opened them up and blew.

Some sort of dust whipped up from her open palms and swirled around the space in front of her before dissipating. It would have looked impressive had I not been more concerned by the angry, chomping faces headed in my direction.

I retreated as far as I could but it was a small room and my back was against the wall before I knew it. Jenny was pressed up against the wall next to me and for the first time since we met, which admittedly was all of 3 minutes ago, she looked stressed.

Two faces on stalks were moving towards me, their teeth gnashing, drool dribbling from their chins, well from Issy Ford's chin anyway, the other face belonged to someone I didn't recognise and he had a long hipster beard so the drool was just kind of sitting there on the beard. It struck me that if the beardy face reached me first I'd be slathered in drool before the teeth made contact and I was surprised by how much this bothered me given I was probably going to be eaten anyway.

Then a book flew off the shelves and hit beardy-face in the ... face.

"It's working!" cried Jenny.

I was too busy ducking under Issy Ford's lunging bite attack to really take this in and then I noticed that a third face, we'll call this one Miss Orange Face (because she had a particularly orange face, presumably either a result of too much fake tan, or an overdose of Sunny D in the nineties. Look at me being all judgemental in my descriptions like what proper writers do), was heading right for Jenny's jugular and she was too busy looking at the books throwing themselves off shelves to notice.

"Look out!" I shouted and surprised myself by also taking action and pulling Jenny out of the way of the orange-skinned attacker.

It wasn't much of a save as Miss Orange Face had cornered us now and Issy Ford was right there next to her. They probably would have eaten us if not for the thing that leapt from the pages of that first book that had hit beardy-face in the ... face. It sailed through the air and clamped its jaws around the stalk that Miss Orange Face was attached to, severing it in one bite. Issy watched her compatriot drop to the floor then screeched that horrible screech again before another creature leapt from another book and bit Issy free of her stalk too. The creatures, now I had a chance to take in what was happening, were the bookworms from Jenny's book.

The worms looked like what tapeworms look like in my nightmares of what a tapeworm is, not what they actually look like which is probably quite different. They were a pale, fleshy colour and had this round hole for a mouth that was lined with really nasty-looking teeth. There were a dozen of them in the room already, crawling from books that had fallen from the shelves.

"Bookworms!" shouted Jenny with genuine glee, "You're a genius."

The faceplant had been slowed down but was still sending more faces on stalks into the room, which were in turn unceremoniously munched by the bookworms. That said, I wasn't entirely sure we were safe from the bookworms either, which is why I haven't commented on Jenny referring to me as a genius. A couple of them were slithering across the floor towards us and one even lunged for my foot as I moved it out of the way.

"You'd think bookworms would be cuter," I mused, although this was clearly not the time for musing another of my talents is being able to muse oblivi-ously at the worst possible moment, "Less snappy."

Jenny seemed to agree and grabbed my hand. To-gether we bounded over the advancing bookworms, ducked beneath the remaining faces that had con-gregated outside the door, and made it back out onto the relative safety of the third floor.

7: A POST-STRUCTURAL ANALYSIS OF ROSEMARY'S BABY

The third floor was everything but safe by this point. The faceless students were still running around aimlessly and there were more of them now, the others presumably drawn by the face-plant and the precious faces they seemed to want so badly. They were reaching to grab the faces on stalks, which had also multiplied as the plant grew bigger by the second. The ceiling tiles had pretty much all come down now but rather than the usual network of pipes, ducts and wiring you would expect to see above a suspended ceiling there were just the undulating vines and stalks of the gigantic faceplant as it continued its hostile takeover of the library. At the same time, every book on the shelves was shaking violently and bookworms were emerging from the books that fell to the floor. Most of the stalks and a few of the faceless students already had bookworms hanging off them and once those teeth had found flesh they weren't letting go anytime soon.

I don't think I've done a good enough job of describing how bat-shit crazy it was. Just take a second to picture it – students without faces running around aimlessly trying to grab angry, bitey faces attached to a giant plant growing from the ceiling, which in turn is being munched on by prehistoric worm creatures coming out of books. Start by imagining just one of each of those things, okay? Got it? Now multiply everything you've just imagined by a hundred and then add some movement and chaos and screeching and you probably still won't be anywhere close to imagining how insane this was but at least you'll have an image that's a bit insane and the rest you will just have to take my word for.

"This didn't really go according to plan," said Jenny, winning the prize for understatement of the century, which I would have offered to present to her but I didn't feel like we knew each other well enough for sarcasm yet and I was scared of offending her because she still seemed like my best and only chance of escaping the library with my face intact.

Jenny was flicking through the book again.

"Can't you just, I don't know, undo everything?" I offered.

I can't believe Jenny hadn't thought of this before but apparently she hadn't as it was only upon me suggesting it that she flicked to the very last page of the book.

"Here we are! I just promise my soul to this dude and we're sorted."

I kicked an approaching bookworm away and then looked down at the page she was showing me. There was another woodcut image but this one showed the silhouette of a large figure with what appeared to be a pair of twisted, asymmetrical horns on its head. And then I registered what Jenny had actually said.

"Your soul?" I repeated, more to myself than to her.

Here are the questions that were running through my head at that particular moment –

Did I believe in the concept of a soul?

If I did believe in a soul and I knew what it was, was exchanging one's soul for favours a good idea?

I felt like I knew the concept of selling souls from films and wanted to use one as an example, but which films feature the character selling their soul?

Is it one of those things that we think is a massive cliché because it happens in films all the time but when you try to think of films where it happens, especially when you're trying to think in the middle of a crisis and don't have time to check the IMDB, you realise it doesn't happen in as many films as you thought?

Does it happen in *Rosemary's Baby?*

Does John Cassavetes sell his soul in *Rosemary's Baby* or is it not explicitly stated?

He makes a deal with the Satan worshippers, that's for sure, and his acting career takes off as a result but surely the bargaining chip is his wife's fertility, not his soul, but then does he forfeit his soul anyway by virtue of being a friend to Satan worshippers?

What is a soul anyway?

Do I have a soul?

If I do have a soul can I sell mine and what can I get for it?

Presumably, if a soul is something you can sell to Satan for anything you want then someone else would be willing to pay a high price on eBay but does that go against eBay's guidelines?

How does one take a photo of one's soul for the eBay listing?
Why aren't people selling their souls on eBay all the time, or maybe they are?

Will Jenny, this person I don't know, have seen *Rosemary's Baby* and is it a strong enough example to use when voicing concern about selling one's soul? After all, things seemed to work out okay for Rosemary in the end. Although it is another film made by Roman Polanski who also made the Johnny Depp/Skeletor film and you don't want to reference too many Polanski films when you've just met someone in case they think you only like films made by sex offenders, which is pretty much all films made by men between 1970 and 2020 anyway so best not to reference too many films at all other than really old ones. Although that doesn't make sense because it was Jenny in the present I was talking to about that one Johnny Depp film so I wouldn't actually be having this thought in the past which calls into question this whole bit. This is what happens when I try to be too clever.

Still, it's worth asking, are there any films in which a soul is sold that aren't made by sex offenders?

THE LIBRARY OF LOST SOULS

Before I could answer any of these questions or even utter the words of warning, "Don't be a *Rosemary's Baby*", which didn't make sense but were the words I was leaning towards, Jenny pulled me out of the way of a particularly aggressive bookworm that was about to chomp down on my ankle.

"We need to get off this floor," she said.

She was right, we really did.

8: AN UNLIKELY LOCATION FOR A SHOWDOWN

"Toilets!" I shouted as we ran out into the stairway.

The gents toilets on the 2nd floor were my sanctuary. I may have implied that the library was my sanctuary and that is true, it was, but when the library became too much and I needed sanctuary from the silence and overwhelming sense of inadequacy invoked by being in a room with actual students doing actual work I would retreat to the 2nd-floor toilets. The gents toilets were on every other floor so we had to go down one floor, I mean obviously, at a time of crisis we could have used the ladies on the 3rd floor, technically all the toilets were supposed to be unisex anyway but the temporary signage looked so shoddy nobody could really tell whether it was genuine or the work of student activists. I say nobody, I mostly meant me. I was still too scared to go into the lady's toilets in case I'd misread the situation and became embroiled in a conflict when all I really wanted to do was hide in a cubicle and listen to podcasts for an hour or so. If the toilets in the library became a source of embarrassing memories then I wouldn't have any sanctuary from the library itself and would pretty much have to stop going altogether so as much as I supported the change to gender-inclusive toilets I was going to stick to my beloved 2nd floor former gents, partly through habit but also to avoid my own crippling insecurities. Once proper signage had been installed, I would have revised my position, but as you're about to find out I wouldn't have to worry about proper signage in the library toilets for much longer. No one would.

Sorry, spoiler alert.

Sorry, I'm supposed to say that before the spoiler.

Luckily the clanging and screeching sounds coming from the 3rd-floor toilets suggested they were already occupied by part of the faceplant and/or faceless students and/or bookworms so going in was never an option. We ran down one floor and dived into the 2nd floor former gents, now possibly unisex, loos, which Jenny stormed into without any hesitation proving I'd been overthinking everything as usual.

Jenny laid the book out between two washbasins. I mean, not quite between them, there wasn't enough space, but it sort of overlapped the raised lip of each basin and then dipped in the middle. This is why I shouldn't be writing this, all I wanted to say is that Jenny opened the book and laid it out across two sinks and I know exactly what that looks like but I just can't find the words to describe such an arrangement with a modicum of elegance, and yet I'm happy to use the word "modicum" which for all I know isn't a real word and is just one of those things that people think makes them sound clever but actually comes from something else with an entirely different meaning. Oh, okay I checked and it does apparently mean "a small quantity of a particular thing", which is exactly what I meant it to mean so maybe I'm actually really good at writing after all.

The book was open at the page with the creepy, horned figure and I remembered that before I was distracted by our quest for a modicum (my new favourite word) of security, I was actually intending to voice my concern about Jenny's plan.

"Okay, I clearly know nothing about all this," is how I opened, because it was the truth, "but isn't it a bit weird that everything you've looked for in that book, even the most random thing, has been right there?"

That was a genuine concern, by the way, it just took my brain a while to get there. I had entered the library as someone for whom faceless students, bookworm, and faceplants were not things that existed and nor were they things that could be conjured. I now knew these things most certainly did exist and yet I couldn't help questioning their existence. Is that how magic works? I thought magic was the thing where you point somewhere else and then hide the coin in your palm and it looks like magic because you have more patience than me and practiced it a million more times than I did in the mirror. If magic exists, real magic, would it be as simple as thinking of a thing and looking it up in a book that has all the things? I realise now that my concerns on this subject would have been a better way to open this section as opposed to my toilet etiquette worries but this is where we are.

Jenny looked at me, mind clearly blown, and shouted, "Yes! You are absolutely correct. What a fool I've been. You, a stranger I've only just met who knew nothing of magic and bookworms and faces on plants 5 minutes ago, have managed to point out an obvious truth that I had not wanted to confront because I wanted to believe it was my skill and talent as a conjurer that had brought forth these homunculi and not the twisted machinations of a cursed book!"

She didn't say that but I just wanted to hear how it sounded.

Instead, she was looking at one of the cubicles, distracted and not even really listening to me.

"Why is that cubicle on fire?"
I should have been annoyed at this clear ignorance of the potential solution I had laid out before Jenny (figuratively laid out, not awkwardly laid out on top of the lips of two sinks) but the answer to her question was something so unexpected I momentarily forgot my concerns. The answer to Jenny's question was Daniel Middleton.

Spoiler alert, sorry.

We were looking at the cubicle and there was smoke billowing out of the top. Then the toilet flushed and the door opened and there he was, my future husband, standing smoking a joint like it's the most natural thing in the world (it was a fact well-documented in student forums that the smoke alarms in the gents on the 2nd floor of the library hadn't worked since 1986).

We stared at Daniel. Daniel stared at us. Then he realised he hadn't zipped up his flies.

"Oh, sorry," he said as if that was the reason we were staring at him, but it wasn't. I was staring because of all the toilets in all the world he had to wander into mine. Also, we were staring at him because he was the first person we'd seen in the library who still had a face. He must have come in around the same time I did after Jenny had done the face-taking spell. Had I been a few seconds later we might have bumped into each other. We might have stood in the doorway chatting ("Oh, you come here to smoke weed in the second-floor gents? What a coincidence! I come here to hide from everyone and pretend I'm a real student when really I just look for weird books") and realised we had more in common than we first thought and that neither of us really wanted to be in the library that night so we'd go for a drink instead and it would be the beginning of something beautiful and wonderful and I would never have met Jenny and never have known about magic and real-life book worms and faces on stalks like the one that was emerging from the toilet behind Daniel's head and looming over him with an open mouth, about to snap.

Daniel turned to see what we were looking at. This was my chance. I could leap in, pull him away from the biting face, with a cry of, "No! Take me instead!"

Then Jenny would save me because it was all her fault and she knew that so she would have to sacrifice herself and that would break the spell and me and Daniel would walk away into the sunrise having survived.

Daniel was making a noise like he was trying to scream like he'd seen in films but had never actually done a scream before so was still kind of trying it out. The face was coming for him, mouth open, drool dripping from hungry lips. Daniel had been about to light up again but as he staggered backwards he dropped both his joint and lighter then turned to run. The face on the plant was nearly on top of him, he wasn't going to make it. This was my moment. I took two strides forward then jumped past Daniel and into the air, wrapping my arms around the stalk and bringing it down to the floor. I lay there with my arms and legs wrapped around the wriggling stalk with the face trying its hardest to bite me and I looked up for Daniel Middleton's grateful smile of approval.

All I saw was the door to the toilets swinging shut, signalling his exit and then I saw Jenny looking at the book again.

"No!" I shouted, because that's what you do in moments like this, you shout "No!" at the person about to do the stupid and dangerous thing, "There has to be another way!"

Jenny ignored me and whispered the words from the book into her cupped hands. She opened her palms and blew a cloud of black, ash-like dust at her reflection in the mirror. In an instant, the surface of the mirror lost its reflective sheen and clouded over with a thick, black mould. In the centre, at the heart of the mould, something was moving.

"This may have been a mistake," said Jenny, and I would have agreed but I was rather distracted by the face still trying to eat me.

I needed to release the stalk to help Jenny but I knew the moment I did so I was face-food so I sort of kicked it away from me with my feet then shuffled across the floor. The face reared up on its stalk like a snake about to strike. I noticed at that moment that the stalk was still halfway through the door of the cubicle so I stood up, grabbed the top of the door with both hands, and slammed it shut. The door bounced off the stalk without appearing to have caused much damage but the agonised shriek from the face suggested otherwise. I pulled on the door again, slamming it into the stalk twice more before the face backed away, retreating into the cubicle and freeing me up to see how Jenny was doing.

The small thing that was moving in the centre of the mouldy reflection in the mirror was now a bigger thing. When the undulating mould shifted enough for us to see it was clear that the figure in the reflection was the horned creature from the book and it was moving ever closer. Jenny was staring at the creature, frozen with indecision.

I was not frozen with indecision; I was nobly accepting my fate.

That's not what it looked like, Jen, but if you want to write your own chronicle one day and describe how you think you reacted then please go ahead.

That's when I had the idea to prove to Jenny what was going on, or at least what I thought was going on. If my theory proved to be incorrect then what I did next would appear rather random.

Grabbing the book from the sink I said, "I have an idea! How about a spell where I have cheese for a head and you're a giant rabbit?"

I opened the book to a random page and showed it to Jenny. There, much to my satisfaction was wood-cut image of a figure who looked a bit like me but with a huge block of Swiss cheese for a head standing next to a goth rabbit wearing a black dress and stripy tights.

She looked up from the book, her eyes widening as they met mine and she said, "It's the fucking book!"

It was the perfect "I told you so" moment and it was ruined entirely by the sound of cracking toilet bowls, splitting pipes, shattered urinals, splintered wood and water gushing into the air as a bunch more faces on stalks pushed themselves up through the floor. In case that wasn't enough of a confirmation that we were well and truly fucked, the faceless students chose this moment to reveal they too had tracked us down, pushing open the door and barging into the room with bookworms slithering and snapping around their feet. I felt a couple of the stalks wrap themselves around my legs and looked down to see two angry faces looking up at me with bared teeth. I looked up at Jenny and saw that behind her a clawed hand was emerging from the mould on the mirror, reaching out to grab her.

Jenny appeared to have given up and who could blame her? She clearly did know about magic and stuff but I could tell even she hadn't been prepared for the carnage the book had unleashed upon the library. As the faceplant dragged me back towards more biting faces I almost started to laugh. In my wildest predictions, I never would have guessed that this would be how my shortish life would end. Imagine trying to explain it to fourteen-year-old me? Actually, that was a bad age to pick. Fourteen-year-old me would probably have welcomed the news of his death in any form and would have accepted the sorry tale of his future with a satisfied nod. Me at seven? No, seven-year-old me would not have been able to take it seriously. Maybe I was the perfect age for this to happen in that I could appreciate both the tragedy of my life being cut short and also the comedy in the manner of which I faced my final moments?

My melancholy thoughts were interrupted by a sharp pain from my left calf and I looked down to see one of the faces biting down. My attention was then pulled away by a flash of movement ahead of me. Jenny had picked up Daniel's lighter from the floor and then she reached into her bag and retrieved my deodorant that had proved so effective on the faceplant earlier.

"The book!" yelled Jenny.

I realised I was still holding it.

"Throw it!"

I was never the best at throwing, or catching for that matter, and being restrained and bitten by faces on stalks didn't help but I managed to kind of fling the book up into the air. Had I known what Jenny was planning I may have aimed a little higher, or at least further away from me.

Jenny held up the lighter, sparked up a flame, and then sprayed the deodorant in what seemed like one fluid movement but in reality was probably an awkward mess as I doubt she'd ever really done anything like that before. In my memory, it was perfect. As the flammable gas hit the flame it became a cloud of fire that consumed the book as it flew through the air. The ancient pages burned quickly and the remains that hit the floor were already charred beyond recognition. Jenny blasted the book with another burst of flame, which was the moment I realised my legs were getting hot.

The stalks of the faceplant were on fire. At first, I thought they had been caught in the burst of Jenny's makeshift flamethrower, but then I glanced behind me to see that the whole plant was aflame. The stalks slackened their grip and I wriggled free then patted out the fire on my trouser legs. It was then that I noticed how silently the faceplant burned given that every other attempt to damage it had caused screeches of agony. It was because the faces on the ends of the stalks were gone. I looked over at the students in the doorway and was relieved to see they now had their faces back. The bookworms at their feet were also on fire. There was one last thing to check, the claw emerging from the mirror, which had retreated and the mirror was slowly returning to normal as well.

That's everything accounted for. Go us!

9: THAT SCENE AT THE END OF FILMS WITH ALL THE AMBULANCES

You know in films there's that last scene where the ambulances and police have turned up and your main characters are sitting there in those shiny space blankets and the one bloke is being carried away on a stretcher but you know he's going to be okay because he's in the sequel or whatever – that's this moment except me and Jenny weren't in the ambulances or on the stretcher and we didn't have shiny space blankets, mostly because we had retreated to a safe distance, or at least safe enough to not be arrested for arson but close enough to be able to watch the library burn to the ground. We were sitting on a grassy hill around half a mile away. I'd picked up Daniel Middleton's discarded joint when we left the toilets with the intention of giving it back to him. Jenny handed me the lighter and I sparked up. It was a night of firsts. First time smoking weed. First experience with magic. First experience with face-plants and bookworms and so on...

Oh fuck, I missed a bit. So, there was the part where we helped all the students make it out, that's important, but I didn't want to dwell on it too much because I don't want it to sound like we were hero-ically running back into the fire to make sure every-one was out. The fire alarm did eventually go off once the fire had spread beyond the 2nd-floor gents and we figured everyone who heard it must know to get out of there so we sort of just held the door open for a few of them until it became unsafe/awkward and then we left the rest of them to it. To be fair, the doors were automatic so we didn't even really have to hold them, we just stood there and made big swooping motions with our arms in case it wasn't obvious that the door was open, which it was, I don't know, we both just felt like we needed to do something. I couldn't say with absolute certainty that everyone made it out alive at that moment but I needed to tell myself that they did because other-wise there was just too much to take in. To be clear, it was all Jenny's fault, if anything I was an innocent victim of circumstance, but I still couldn't help feeling a little like an accomplice.

Anyway, there we were in the doorway directing the confused students with faces outside and then Jenny suddenly stops making the big swooping motions with her arms. She's staring out through the door and there's a man there. He's tall and thin and could have been any age between fifty and seventy-five for all I knew. He was wearing a pinstriped suit and a bowler hat and he was carrying an umbrella. The odd thing about this man was that he didn't seem at all phased by what was going on, he was just watching. I remember when I was in secondary school these two kids arranged to have a fight in the park near the school because if you didn't make a formal arrangement the fight would be broken up really quickly and no one would get properly hurt. So about thirty kids all go to this park to watch the fight but then just as the two kids start shoving and rolling around on the floor and stuff this old man walks over and we all think he's going to break up the fight but he didn't, he just wanted to watch two kids beat the shit out of each other. Which is creepy now I think about it but I always remembered it and then looking at the man in the suit I thought the same thing. Some people just like watching some messed-up shit go down.

That's literally the only significant thing that happened on the way out, then me and Jenny ran for the hills, or hill, and then we got high and watched the library burn.

"My name's Jenny," said Jenny, "Jenny Ringo."

I mean you knew that already because I kept referring to her as Jenny but I'm telling you what she said at that moment because I'm obviously all about accuracy.

"I'm Gavin," I replied because it was my name. Still is, actually.

"You saved my life tonight, Gavin. We have to be best friends forever now."

I should end the story there. It's a nice ending. You can picture it, Jenny and me sitting on the hill with our backs to the camera, silhouetted against the flaming building that consumes the frame. A cute indie ballad with edgy lyrics starts to play, or maybe a twee ukulele cover of a messed up song like "My Shit's Fucked Up" by Warren Zevon but sung by someone with the voice of a twelve-year-old-girl, that kind of thing would start to play and we would fade to black and roll credits.

Here's what happened after the credits rolled. Jenny legged it as soon as she could. I walked back to my room and immediately regretted the joint because I was starting to feel paranoid that it had been laced with PCP because my only other drug-related experience had been listening to Leak Bros. When I eventually made it, I lay on the bed in a foetal position and failed to sleep because of all the fucking horrifying things I'd witnessed that I couldn't get out of my head.

When the sun came up I decided I would hide in my room all day but then I had a call from my Personal Tutor. She called me into her office, I won't describe the journey there but it involved several vomit stops, and then I walked in and she introduced me to two police officers and suddenly I was relieved to have done all my vomiting on the way there. Most of the CCTV from the library had been destroyed but they did manage to retrieve a clip from the camera in the stairway showing me running from the 2nd-floor toilets where the fire had started. Jenny had somehow not been caught on camera, I mean she was there, she's not a vampire although we'll get to them later, she just got caught up in the stampede of students and you could barely see the top of her head in the recording. It looked bad. It looked like I'd started the fire then made a run for it.

What was I supposed to say? Jenny wasn't a student at the university, there would be no record of her being there and even if there had been, I wouldn't know what to tell them about her or even if I wanted to tell them anything. At this point I could still remember Jenny telling me we were best friends forever now and although I didn't totally understand what had happened, I knew Jenny had been trying to fix it.

Later I would change my mind because as I was about to find out, Jenny had ruined my life. I couldn't explain what had happened and there wasn't enough evidence to take it any further but the faculty wanted me out. My tutor told me quite frankly that she thought I was responsible and that she would use my poor academic performance as an excuse if she had to but one way or another I was going home.

And that, dear reader, was the end of my academic career.

Sometime later I was at the bus stop. I didn't know where I was going, I'd let five buses come and go. I hadn't gone back to my room for my stuff. I felt sick again but it was the kind of feeling sick that comes after you've made a really bad life choice and you can't actually vomit the regret out to make yourself feel better so the feeling of nausea just sits there, much like I was sitting there at the bus stop, with nowhere to go.

And then there was Jenny.

"I got a job!" she shouted as she walked on over with a huge grin.

"I got kicked off my course for starting the fire in the library and now I have nowhere to live!"

"That's great! Oh wait, what did you say?"

I explained the police, the lack of explanation, my lack of a future.

"Oh," was Jenny's comforting response, "Bugger."

"My loan has been cancelled, I have to move out of halls but I can't go back home, I just can't."

I know, I could have gone home. It would have been awkward and awful and would likely have led to depression and probably would not have ended well but it was an option, just not one I ever wanted to consider.

"You can move in with me," offered Jenny with sincerity.

"You must be joking," I said because I felt like it was too soon to stop pretending to be mad at her but really, I was ready to agree immediately.

"Look, I can't help feeling partly responsible—"

"Try fully responsible! I don't even know what happened last night, I just know it was your fault and now everything is ruined! What are you even doing here?"

Is what I said but what I was thinking was, "Please let me move in with you. I'm just doing a bit of a performance because it really was your fault and I don't want to let you off the hook on that, but don't let me distract you from the original offer."

"I came to look for you. I told you, we're best friends forever now."

I had wanted to show a bit of remorse but this was too much remorse and I was possibly going to cry so I turned away, which looked more dramatic than intended.

"I'm sorry about what happened," she persevered, "I know I can't make it up to you but the least I can do is offer you a place to stay while you figure things out."

I nodded, hoped the tears had dried enough then turned around and moved in for a hug but then realised we still didn't know each other that well so I backtracked and morphed the hug into a handshake at the last minute, which looked ten times more awkward than whatever you're imagining it looked like.

We shook hands and we headed over to my room to pick up my stuff to take over to Jenny's new place.

Because she hadn't moved in yet.

Because until that morning Jenny had been sleeping on the streets, or on that particular morning, underneath the pier on Brighton seafront.

Because her new job was only given to her that morning and came with a place to live.

And guess who offered her this new job and place to live?

If you guessed the creepy old guy in the suit and bowler hat who was standing outside the library when we were leaving you would have guessed right.

But you won't have guessed that because I don't think I set him up properly because I was trying to be clever about it and then I almost forgot to introduce him entirely.

10: MOVING DAY

We borrowed a shopping trolley from Tesco, wheeled it over to the building where I lived then I went in, opened my window and passed my collection of Retro Gamer magazines, my old SNES and my shitty old TV out to Jenny. I loaded up the trolley with clothes and boring stuff I'm not going to list here (but now that feels weird because I started with a list, so it was my toothbrush and other bathroom items and ... no this really is stuff you don't need to know. Imagine you had to move house in a hurry and you had to load everything you might need for the immediate future into a shopping trolley. Got it? All that stuff you just thought of, that's what I put in the trolley).

I tried to leave a bit of space for Jenny's stuff but she kept pointing at things in my room and asking if I needed them so she was basically complicit in me taking up all the space. I should probably have been asking more questions, like where was her new place? What were the public transport connections like? What kind of area was it in? I didn't ask those questions because the whole experience was a bit weird and vaguely thrilling like we were fugitives on the run from the law and were having to get out of town in a hurry. Except we weren't getting out of town because Jenny's new place was in Brighton, or at least I assumed it was. She didn't seem too sure. That's the thing, if I had asked any questions it would've been pointless because Jenny didn't really know much more about where she was moving to than I did.

On the way into town we mostly relived the events of the previous night, but as we pushed the trolley along the Brighton seafront I began to notice reality again. It was the middle of the day and the beach was bustling with day drinkers, as it often was. I'd always been a bit jealous of the day drinkers at the bars along the seafront, not because I wanted to join them particularly but because they always seemed so happy like they knew something about life I still hadn't figured out. I think, despite my reservations about drinking and socialising and people in general, I think I secretly wanted to be them and I always thought I'd figure out how to be someday. It was this thought that made me consider my current situation again so I began to ask more questions.

Here's a transcript so I don't have to keep writing "I said," and "she replied," or even worse, "I exclaimed," which is something people only do in books, no one "exclaims" in real life, if you were at a party and someone started "exclaiming" stuff you'd think they were a dickhead. So we're doing it like this instead –

G (that's me): Is your new place in Hove? We seem to be heading that way.

J (that's Jenny): It's not in Hove.

G: Oh. Where is it, then? Portslade? Southwick?

J: I'll know it when I see it.

G: What? (I may not have said this, I may have used an expression or perplexed intake of breath to indicate my ... perplexion)

J: That's what he said. He said I'll know it when I see it.

G: Right. Are we going to your place first?

Don't worry, we'll come back to the flat. I still didn't know Jenny that well at this point so our conversations were a bit awkward and sensing she was a little irritated with my questions I decided to change the subject. This is like literally how the conversation happened, I'm being proper authentic and stuff.

J: I don't have a place.

G: Right.

Awkward pause. Actually, there were a lot of these, I'm not going to put them all in. Just imagine an awkward pause wherever you think there should be one and then multiply them by a thousand and you'll be halfway close to the actual number of awkward pauses in this particular interaction.

G: Where were you staying?

J: Anywhere I could.

G: But like, specifically where? So last night, for example. Where did you stay last night?

J: Last night I slept on the beach under the pier.

She actually pointed across to the pier because we were nearby.

G: Oh, shit. You're homeless?

J: I have a home.

G: Right. Where's that then?

J: I'll know it when I see it.

G: Oh, I get it, you didn't have a home but you do now.

J: You ask a lot of fucking questions.

G: Sorry.

Awkward pause. Sorry, I had to put that one in because it would feel weird without it.

G: Actually, I'm not sorry. Can we talk about this? I have no idea who you are!

J: I'm Jenny. Jenny Ringo.

G: Yes, but where did you come from?

J: Can't you tell from the accent?

I couldn't tell, she didn't really have one. She didn't sound northern, but she didn't sound particularly southern either.

G: Leeds?

I guessed Leeds because Neil in one of my seminars said he came from Leeds but he sounded really posh so no one believed him so I wondered if there was a secret posh Leeds accent.

J: Not from Leeds. Sorry, I'm a bit distracted. I need to concentrate if I'm going to find this flat.

G: Is the flat real?

J: Yes.

G: How do you know?

At this point, Jenny tossed me a set of keys. There were two keys, one rusted to the point it didn't look like it would open anything and another that was shiny and new. There was also a silver tag attached to the ring with the number '2' engraved in it. I mean, aside from the rusty key it looked legit. I tossed them back.

G: Okay, so you picked up the keys from the letting agent but they didn't give you an address?

J: No, he said I wouldn't need it.

G: Who said that?

J: The man. From the council. I thought I explained all this?

G: You haven't explained anything!

Jenny stopped, clearly annoyed but as you can tell from the above really I should have been annoyed and I kind of was but I wasn't very good at display-ing frustration with people in the moment, particu-larly people I'd only just met. She sat on a bench.

J: This is what happened. After the library, I ran as far away as I could. I didn't want to have to answer any questions. I'd been staying in London and had come down for the interview but I didn't feel like going back right away. I'd never been to Brighton be-fore. I wandered around the town for a bit. I tried a few bars until I found a contingent of spooky folk dressed like me. They were nice. One of them, I want to say her name was Beatrice, but it probably wasn't her real name, she probably just thought it sounded witchy, Beatrice bought me a drink. We went to a club on the seafront. There were a couple of bands playing. We danced. I did a line in the loos, which isn't something I'd normally do but Beatrice offered and it was one of those nights where you just do all the things. I wanted to forget who I was for a few hours. I wanted to forget about the library and the faceless people and the plant and the worms and the fire and the danger of death and the implications of all of that. I wanted to be a normal goth in her twenties in Brighton with her goth friends dancing and laughing and forgetting. Beatrice's boyfriend came to meet us, I don't remember his name, I was pissed and high and a bit of a mess, I just remember he was really tall. We'd left the club and Beatrice said I could stay over at her place, which sounded like a great idea except my legs had stopped working so I asked if her tall boyfriend could put me on his shoulders, which he did because he was pissed too. The thing is he wasn't actually that much taller than me and it was a bit awkward and then I threw up in his hair and he was pretty unhappy with me for that. Beatrice wasn't too happy either, which is when I realised I didn't actually know these people, I'd just done too good a job of forgetting. I left Beatrice trying to clean my sick out of her boyfriend's hair and I set off along the beach. I guess I just sort of passed out under the pier, although it was kind of a decision.

I woke up feeling awful but hadn't choked on my own vomit or anything like that so it was all good. This man was standing there. He was at the library as well, do you remember? He was tall and skinny and wearing a pin-stripe suit and a bowler hat, like a cartoon of a man going to work in the City in the 1940s. Or like Mr. Benn in a movie adaptation if Tim Burton had directed it. Sorry, that's an old reference. My pop culture knowledge is a bit fucked, I'll explain one day but it's a long story. He was holding my CV in his hand, I guess it had been in my bag from when I had the interview. When he spoke it sounded like an old-fashioned horror movie star, like somewhere between Vincent Price and Christopher Lee, which I guess is Peter Cushing but he didn't really sound like Peter Cushing.

"Does this belong to you?"

He was smiling. He seemed friendly.

I nodded and then I think I apologised. I assumed he was going to have a go at me for littering, which made me laugh because I kind of felt like I was the litter really, like I'd littered myself. I'm not sure why I laughed, that's kind of fucked-up. I thought he was going to fine me or something, that's the thing, so I apologised again.

"No no, you misinterpret my intention. You see, only a moment ago I was speaking to a dear friend about a rather dire resource situation at his place of work. Naturally, I agreed to inform him if I happened across any suitable candidates, and the next thing I know your curriculum vitae lands at my feet. So, what do you think?"

It took me a moment to understand that he was offering me a job. I had to check.

"Of course! Coincidences like this don't happen every day now, do they? When we are so blessed we must be sure to make the most of them."

I almost accepted on the spot. Despite how the night had ended I had come to quite like Brighton in my short time here and I was looking for an excuse to stay, however, I decided I should probably ask what kind of job it was so I did.

"Oh, nothing too taxing. Whatever one does in an office these days. It would suit someone looking for a … grown-up job. You are a grown-up aren't you, Jennifer?"
Which is a weird thing to say but as you are aware I'm quite used to weirdness and people saying weird things doesn't always stand out to me because of all the other weird shit.

"You can start tomorrow, yes?"

I agreed and I shook his hand and then I thought I'd push my luck and I asked him whether he also knew someone with a flat to rent. I was half-joking, but it turns out he did. He gave me a key and told me I'd know the place when I found it.

After that I pulled myself together and realised I needed to tell someone because that's what you do with good fortune, you tell someone else about it. I couldn't tell Beatrice, she probably still hates me, so I decided to come and find you and now we're moving in together.

G: If we can find the place.

J: Yes, exactly.

A few things to mention here. Firstly, I am fully

aware that Jenny just did that annoying thing that people do in books where they're telling someone about a thing that happened but then they remember the conversation verbatim, which never happens, but then this whole chapter is a bit like that so you'll just have to deal with it. Secondly, her story makes no sense and explains nothing really, I still had no idea where we were going but she seemed to think she'd said enough and I didn't want to press her on it, to be honest, I kind of wanted a cup of tea so I decided to give her the benefit of the doubt and we continued walking.

The conversation also continued, as follows –

G: Somehow, I can't really see you working in some stuffy office photocopying spreadsheets.

J: I don't know if the office is stuffy yet, maybe it's one of those nice modern offices where there's a PlayStation room and sofas instead of desks and they have a tiki theme day every other Friday.

G: Maybe. What did you do for a job before?

J: I haven't had many jobs, really.

G: I sort of imagined you'd do something magicky, like working in a curiosity shop.

J: I'm not doing that anymore.

G: The magic or the working in a curiosity shop?

J: I don't think curiosity shops are a thing.

G: You're not doing magic anymore?

J: You sound disappointed.

I was disappointed. Jenny was going to be my witch friend. I'd talk about her at dinner parties with my new friends I was going to make and then one day they would meet her and she would do tricks, except she'd do old-school sleight-of-hand stuff like pulling coins out of people's ears and then we'd all laugh because my stories had been really convincing but then me and Jenny would wink at each other because we knew she really did know magic. Looked like it was just going to be the one story.

J: How can you possibly be disappointed after what you saw last night? I nearly got you killed.

G: Maybe you just need to get better at it?

Jenny reached into her tattered bag, which by now I knew probably held all her worldly possessions, which turned out to mostly be notebooks.

She walked over to a litter bin and, fully aware of what a drama queen moment this was, exclaimed (it's allowed when people are being drama queens), "I'm done with magic."

I can't really say why I did what I did next. In the moment I told myself it was because that one notebook on the top was a straightforward paper spiral-bound notebook and it should really go in a recycling bin. Later I told myself it was because I just couldn't stand the idea of Jenny putting all that time into filling the notebook only to throw it away. If I was being honest with myself I thought that maybe she would thank me for doing it. If I was being genuinely honest with myself I would admit that I took it because I believed in magic now and I wondered if maybe there was something in there I could use, and yes, I'm ashamed to admit I did try but I'm not going to talk about that. Yet. Anyway, I took that one notebook from the bin and slipped it into the trolley with my stuff when Jenny wasn't looking.

We didn't talk much after that, we just walked along the seafront. If you want to follow on a map we were walking West, so from Brighton into Hove, then into Portslade, then Southwick, I guess, and after that I'm not sure where we were but it was somewhere I'd never been. I was beginning to question Jenny's "I'll know it when I see it" idea when suddenly –

"That's it!"

We were looking at this large, creepy Victorian building (I'm saying Victorian, I have no idea, it was old and looked like it was from the period where all buildings were made out of boring). I couldn't work out how many storeys it had as we had ended up standing too close to see to the top but it seemed really tall. The building also seemed really out of place compared to the quiet, residential street it was situated on like it had just been built in the middle of all these normal houses rather than the other way around. Also, it looked creepy, did I mention that? The creepiness was quite impressive as we were there on a bright, sunny morning with clear blue skies overhead and yet it still exuded (posh word, had to Google it first to check what it meant) creepiness, like creepiness was running through the pipes instead of hot water.

"Are you sure?"

I knew she was sure, it just felt like the right thing to say and secretly I was hoping she really wasn't sure and that there was a nice, cottagey-type place in the middle of a field around the corner and there would be rabbits in the field and a hill with a tree where I could sit and read like what people used to do in olden times before Netflix. That was the place I wanted and I wondered if spooky Mr. Benn had given me a key and told me I'd know it when I saw it would I have found somewhere a little less creepy?

Jenny didn't answer my question, obviously knowing I knew she knew she was sure. She tried the rusty key in the lock. I half-expected it to break off in the lock and was fully prepared to say, "Oh well, that's that then" as we walked away in search of somewhere more normal to live, but it didn't break. The key slid into the lock, Jenny turned it and with a simple click, the door was unlocked. She pushed the large front door open.

"Are you coming?"

I nodded then pushed my trolley in through the door into a small lobby area.

There were stairs leading up to the flats and a door marked "Private", which presumably led to where all the technical stuff was, you know, boilers and pumps and pipes and things like that.

The lobby had a smell. It smelled of old.

I was going to say something insipid (had to Google again, think it's what I mean, sure, why not?) like, "Seems nice," or ... Probably just "Seems nice" as I couldn't really think of anything else to say but luckily I didn't have to because there was a noise from behind the "Private" door and to be honest, 24 hours ago I would have dismissed the noise as some kind of normal household noise but as a newly converted witness to the impossible I would describe the noise as a growl.

I looked at Jenny.

"Probably just pipes," she said because having turned her back on magic 15 minutes ago she was suddenly full muggle.

I was going to say that out loud when there was another noise, the sound of the front door slamming shut behind us.

It was a sound so deafeningly loud and so incredibly final that it seems like the door would never open again. It was too late to do anything about it by then. We were inside and it wouldn't be too long before we discovered just how final the sound of that door slamming really was, but you don't want to hear about that now. After I learned about the existence of magic via an encounter with faceless students, a giant faceplant, and angry bookworms I needed to sit down and not do anything for a month until the horror of it all had really sunk in, by which time there was far worse stuff to worry about, but I'll get to all that later.

JENNY AND GAVIN
WILL RETURN IN
*THE HOUSEWARMING
PARTY FROM HELL...*

IF YOU ENJOYED THIS BOOK...

Please visit **www.jennyringo.com** and sign up to the mailing list to be notified of future releases.

On signing up to the list you will receive a confirmation email with links to three Jenny Ringo films.

ABOUT THE AUTHOR

Chris Regan

Chris is a writer and filmmaker whose feature screenwriting credits include London Heist, Ten Dead Men and Paintball Massacre. He also created the controversial transmedia horror series Paz vs. Stuff.

The Library of Lost Souls is his first book.

Printed in Great Britain
by Amazon

46998486R00069